THE MYSTERY OF
THE HEADLESS TIGER

THE MYSTERY OF
THE HEADLESS TIGER

STEVE SWANSON

ZondervanPublishingHouse
Grand Rapids, Michigan

A Division of HarperCollins*Publishers*

Library of Congress Cataloging-in-Publication Data

ISBN 0-310-39811-8

Edited by David Lambert
Cover design by Chris Gannon
Cover illustration by Doug Knutson
Interior design by Sue Koppenol
Interior illustrations by Tim Davis

Printed in the United States of America

94 95 96 97 98 99 /❖DH/ 10 9 8 7 6 5 4 3 2 1

 Printed on Recycled Paper

My sincere thanks to
Ruth Geisler, Ron Klug, and Dave Lambert
for early encouragement and help,
and to Shelley Sateren for her many
critiques and suggestions.

Contents

"We need an adventure," Penny said, adjusting her Captain Wizard T-shirt underneath her jacket as she leaned her mountain bike against our garage.

"No kidding," I agreed, carefully leaning my bike next to hers. I was proud of this bike, and I made sure it didn't get dinged or scratched up.

We'd earned these bikes, Penny and I had. Last summer our Middleford police and the FBI rounded up a gang of stolen-gun dealers—right here in our little town—and Penny and I were in the middle of it. It all started when Penny and I were out working for Earthkeepers, our earth-care club. We were hunting for aluminum cans to recycle, and we found a gun in a garbage can—right in the alley behind my house. Before it was over, someone was murdered in our city park, Penny had disappeared from her house, I was shot at, plus I fell off our garage roof and broke my leg. Pretty exciting.

Plus we got new mountain bikes—both of us. The FBI gave them to us for our help.

But compared to that, this fall had been boring us practically to death. Nothing even half as exciting had happened. You get to expect a lot after a summer like that.

And fall was almost over. In fact, as I looked up through the bare trees at the gray sky, I wondered whether we'd get what everyone in town was hoping for—just one more warm weekend.

"Let's go in," I said. "It's cold out here. Mom should be home pretty soon."

Coming home to an empty house after school was getting to feel almost normal. I was learning that the better Mom's real-estate office was doing, the more she would have to be gone.

Last summer, after everyone thought that Penny had been kidnapped from her own house, her dad got scared and hired a live-in cook and gardener—Mr. and Mrs. Chung. Now when Penny goes home there's *always* someone around. My mom can't afford that. If Mom's not home, it's just me. A lot of kids whose parents are divorced get mad about that kind of thing, but to tell the truth, my dad wasn't home that much before the divorce anyway.

But it's funny—even though there's almost always someone around Penny's house, she still comes over here after school. I guess she'd rather have Mom's pat on the cheek at our house than a polite hello from the cook or the gardener at her house. Besides, Mr. and Mrs. Chung usually speak to each other in Korean, which Penny doesn't understand. Yet.

Penny and I fixed celery sticks with chunky peanut butter gobbed into the veined green valleys.

Mom walked in while Penny and I were looking at each other and taking bites at exactly the same time, crunching and laughing.

"You two are nuts," she said. She plopped a grocery bag on the counter and greeted me with a hug and Penny with a pat on the cheek. "I'm glad you're both here," she said. "I have news."

"You found a gun in a garbage can," Penny said, smiling.

"No more of that, thank you," Mom shuddered.

"So what's the news?" I asked, gesturing with my celery stick.

"Have you heard that the Herkenroths are moving?"

"Heard it," I said.

"Me, too," Penny added.

"And do you remember that they were caring for two miles of highway just east of town on Highway 27?"

"I've seen their signs," Penny said. "Adopt-a-Highway."

"It's right out there near your friend Ironman's junkyard," Mom said to me.

"That's the news?" I asked.

"The news is that Mrs. Herkenroth called and offered us that stretch of highway. What do you think?"

"I think that's great," Penny said quickly. "You should take it."

"I did. But there's a problem. Because the Herkenroths have been so busy moving, they haven't done their fall cleanup yet. The highway department wants the autumn cleanup to be finished by this Sunday," Mom said.

"I'll do it," I said.

"And I'll help," said Penny.

"That's why I was so glad you were here, Penny," Mom smiled. "I was almost sure you'd offer. The problem is, I'm tied up almost all weekend. Either we manage to do it somehow, or I'll have to ask Mrs. Herkenroth to give that stretch of highway to someone else."

"Chad and I can do it in time."

"Or if it's too much," I said, "we can get Jay and Pedro to help."

Jay was my second-best friend after Penny. Pedro was new in town and a lot of fun. He moved here from Mexico and knew a lot of neat games they played down there.

"I brought the instructions and the orange jackets home with me. Here." She pulled two of the orange net vests out of a shopping bag and handed them to us. "Try them on," she said. "See how they look. And here are the instructions and warnings," she added, handing each of us a copy.

Penny and I put on the blaze-orange vests and turned in circles. "We look like highway workers," I said.

Penny waved her instruction sheet like a flag. "*Everyone stop!*" she shouted, pretending to flag down traffic.

"Let's go get started right now," I suggested.

"It's too late," Mom warned. "It'll be dark in a half hour. It would be great if you could start first thing in the morning, though."

"We can at least ride out now and have a look, okay?" I asked Penny. When Penny nodded I turned to

Mom. "Can we, Mom?" I pleaded. "Then I'll ride home with Penny so she gets there in time for dinner."

"Oh, all right. But wear your helmets—and you watch out on that highway," Mom said in a stern voice. "Drivers can't see well at dusk."

We jumped on our bikes and took off, riding side by side so we could talk.

"Last spring we saw the Herkenroths out cleaning the ditches," I said between puffing breaths. "Mom and I were hauling a load of cans to Ironman Kenyon's junkyard. We stopped to say hello and Mom asked Mrs. Herkenroth what it was like to clean road ditches."

"What did she say?" Penny asked.

"She said you find some pretty weird stuff."

"That's the exciting part," Penny grinned.

"She said you find some yucky stuff, too—like dirty diapers."

"Oh, yuk." Penny wrinkled her freckled nose.

"Yuk or not, we have to clean up everything," I said. "Even diapers!"

We made it the ten blocks to the Herkenroths' stretch of highway and, since there were no cars, we kept on riding side-by-side.

But we'd only been riding along the highway for a minute or so when suddenly I was aware of a car coming from behind—fast. I hit the brakes and pulled in behind Penny so we'd be riding single file. "Car coming," I said to her. "Watch out." We got as far over on the edge of the road as we could. I checked the car in my helmet mirror—definitely speeding.

Just as the car zoomed past us, something about as big as a head of cabbage flew out of the window. It zipped right in front of Penny's nose and landed in the ditch with a thud.

Penny slammed on her brakes so hard I almost crashed into her. She looked hard toward the ditch where the thing had landed, yelling, "What *was* that?"

"Someone threw something out of that car." I pointed ahead to where the car's tail lights were disappearing. I hadn't gotten much of a look at the car, but I knew it was black and expensive-looking. Maybe a Mercedes.

I heard another car coming fast and turned around to look. It was a Middleford police car—no siren, but its red lights were flashing. Was it chasing that black car?

And if it was, what did the people in the black car throw out while they were being chased?

Without saying a word, we pushed our bikes off the shoulder of the road, laid them against the side of the ditch, and walked down to where the thing might have landed.

"Maybe it sank into the mud." Penny kicked the grass aside with her feet, hunting for the object.

"I wish it weren't so dark." I squinted as I helped search.

"Here's something!" Penny shouted. She reached down for it, but then drew back. "Maybe it's a bomb, Chad. Maybe it will blow up if we touch it."

"Oh, sure. A bomb. Right." I shook my head.

I knelt down and stared at it. But I didn't touch it. "If it *were* a bomb," I said, "it would already have blown up when it hit the ground. I'm picking it up."

"Be careful," Penny warned, backing off.

The package was wrapped in heavy cloth and tied with twine. "Wow—that's heavy!" I said as I lifted it. The wrapping was open on one side. I reached in. Whatever was inside felt like metal and was really cold. "It's cold as ice, Penny," I said. "Feel it."

Penny reached hesitantly inside the package. We both treated it as if it were full of deadly snakes.

Except for the one hole, the package was tightly wrapped, and about the size and shape of a football. I shook it. There were no rattles or movements inside.

"This thing is as heavy as three history books," I said.

"What do you think it is?" Penny asked.

"I don't know." I looked up. It was getting awfully dark. "I think we should take it back to my garage and open it there."

"What if someone comes back for it?" Penny asked.

"Comes *back* for it? They threw it out of their car, right? People don't come back for trash. Besides, finders keepers." I stood my bike up, put the package on the rack in back, and wrapped two bungee cords around it tightly.

As we rode back toward my house we passed the Adopt-a-Highway sign:

The next two miles have been adopted by MILES AND MARIAN HERKENROTH AND FAMILY.

I wondered when they would change the sign and put BUCKWORTH on it. Then I wondered if Penny would want *her* name on it. Buckworth and Palmer.

Sounded like a law firm. Penny's mom and dad probably wouldn't enjoy having their family name on a road sign.

"Too bad you don't have your trailer yet," Penny called back to me.

"Yeah," I said.

Penny knew I wanted a little trailer to hook on behind my bicycle. I wanted it for Earthkeepers projects—collecting cans and bottles, things like that. A trailer would be great for Adopt-a-Highway, too. Whatever recyclables we found in the road ditches, we could put in the trailer and haul back to my garage all by ourselves.

Just before we got to town, a black car passed us, heading back into town. It slowed down beside us, then sped off. It *was* a Mercedes—I was right. I stared after it, wondering who was inside. But it was way too dark to see.

Were the people in that car looking for the package? Had they seen it strapped to my bike? If so, why didn't they stop?

I got my answer to my last question. The police car was right behind them. Instead of chasing the Mercedes, it slowed down beside us. The badge on the right front door was next to Penny's knee as she pedaled. The officer in the passenger seat rolled down the window. "It's too dark to be out on the road," he said to Penny.

"We're on our way home right now," Penny replied.

"Good," he said. "You never know what sorts of people are out on these roads at night. Be careful," he said, waving good-bye as the car pulled away.

When we got back to my house, Penny leaned her bike against the garage and I rolled mine inside, snapping on the light. Penny held the bike as I unstrapped the package and set it on the workbench. "See how heavy it is," I said.

She lifted it. "Wow," she said. When she set it back on the bench, she noticed her watch and gasped. "Oh, no! I forgot. I've got to get home." She turned toward the door, and then suddenly turned back. "But the package! Chad—" She turned toward me and scowled. "Don't you dare open that package without me."

My jaw must have popped open, I was so surprised. "Are you kidding? No way I'm going to wait till tomorrow! Just call your parents and ask if you can stay for five more minutes—"

"I can't," she said. "I'm late already. I have to go. Promise me you won't open it."

"How do you expect me to—"

"Promise!" she demanded, pointing at the package.

Boy, she could be a pain sometimes. "All right," I grumbled. "I promise. I guess I should ride home with you anyway."

She smiled. "Thanks." Then she zipped out of there, and I heard her tires whirring down the alley.

When I got back to the garage, I sat glumly, my chin on my hands, and stared at the package I'd promised not to open.

The Headless Tiger

2

"Now that we've got an adopted highway to keep clean," I told Mom as we ate an early breakfast the next morning, "I need that bicycle trailer more than ever." It was Saturday. I don't much like to sleep late anyway, but I'd never have been able to stay in bed knowing that package was out there waiting to be opened. "Where would you get a bicycle trailer?" Mom asked.

"Guess I'll have to build it," I said.

"The only bicycle trailers I've seen," Mom said, "are the ones that young moms and dads use for pulling little kids around behind their bikes." Mom looked at her watch. "Oh, Chad, I'm sorry. I'm showing the Herkenroth house to some people named Quade from Milwaukee. I have to leave right now. Be sure you and Penny take plenty of trash bags with you. I'll haul your bags of recyclables home for you later. Okay? You and Penny be careful out there on the highway."

"We will," I said. Mom kissed the top of my head as she put on her coat.

Penny showed up about five minutes after Mom left. "I looked in the garage before I came in," she said as she stepped in the back door.

"I waited," I said. But I sure had been tempted the night before to go out and open that package.

"Beat you there," Penny said.

She beat me out the back door, but we squeezed through the garage door at the same time. "Does it still feel really cold?" Penny asked as I reached for the package. She didn't seem to want to touch it. "No," I said, putting my hand inside to see. "It's had all night to warm up."

Penny pushed aside the tools and paint cans on the workbench, clearing a spot in the center. "Come *on*," she insisted.

I hadn't really studied the wrapping the night before. It looked like the thing was wrapped in newspaper, then in cloth, then tied tightly with twine. "Strange cloth," Penny said, touching it lightly with her fingertips. "I've never seen anything like it. It's a little like canvas, but—so rough."

The tan cloth had flecks of dark brown speckles, almost as if it had seeds or weeds woven through it. I picked at the hairy brown knots in the twine for a few moments, then pointed and said, "Would you hand me those tin snips? These knots are too tight."

I cut several of the strings, then peeled back the cloth. Underneath was a thick wrapping of strange newspaper. It was covered with print like any newspaper, but I couldn't read a single word or recognize a single letter. In Spanish or German or French you can at least sound out words even if you don't understand them. This newspaper was in a language I'd never seen before. The letters were as confusing as the Korean magazines over at Penny's house, the ones the Chungs get. "They don't sell newspapers like *that* at Jiffy-Stop," Penny said. "This is getting pretty weird." I unwrapped the newspaper slowly and carefully. Whatever was inside had a lot of paper wrapped tightly around it and wasn't as big as I had first thought. When I had it unwrapped, the object sat in the center of a newspaper nest. It looked like half of an upside-down black banana with legs sticking up in the air.

"What is it?" Penny said, bending over and squinting.

"I don't know. It's upside down," Penny said, reaching for it. "It's a statue of some kind of animal. Look." Penny lifted it out of its wrappings, pushed the paper and cloth aside, and then set the object upright on the bench.

"Oh, cool," I said. "It's a lion or a tiger. But without a head." Penny pushed her hand inside the tiger's body and snapped her fingernail against the inside: *ting, ting.*

"Made out of metal," I said. "Iron, maybe." I poked around in the pile of wrapping, but there wasn't any head inside. "That's all of it. Too bad."

"Why did they paint it black?" Penny asked, pulling her hand out and running it over the surface. If it's iron, maybe to keep it from rusting.?"

"So what happened to the head?"

"Who knows?" I picked it up to study it more carefully. It was painted a dull black, the kind of primer paint you sometimes see on teenagers' cars. "I think it must have been made in two parts," I muttered, running the ball of my finger around the hollow neck.

"They had to do that to make it hollow," Penny said.

"Look at these notches where the head used to hook in," I said. Penny leaned over and looked.

""Look," she said. "It's not painted inside. It looks like gold," she whistled softly.

"Don't we wish. Brass, probably," I said. "But why would someone want to paint a brass tiger with car paint?"

"And why would someone wrap it up so carefully just to throw it away along the road?" Penny added.

"And why wrap it in foreign newspapers?" I asked. "And who took the head off? And why? And where is it?" I set the sculpture back down on the workbench.

"Well—what are we going to do with it?" Penny asked.

"If it had a head, it would be a neat statue. You could polish the paint off and have a shiny brass tiger."

"My mom would probably put it on the mantel," Penny said. "But without a head, it's pretty ugly."

"Without a head it's just junk," I said. "When we get out to our stretch of highway, we can stop at Ironman Kenyon's junkyard. He'll know whether it's brass or not."

"Good idea," Penny said.

I wrapped the tiger loosely in the canvas and bungee-corded it to my bike rack again. "I'm going to take a page from that newspaper with me to church tomorrow," I said, pulling a sheet out of the pile I'd left on the workbench. I smoothed it against my thigh. "We have a couple of retired missionaries. Maybe someone can read that weird language."

"I hope so." Penny nodded.

We pushed our bikes out of my garage and rode toward our section of highway. When we got to the edge of town, we saw the blue "Adopt-a-Highway" sign with the Herkenroth's name on it. We pedaled the two miles to their other sign, then another half-mile to Ironman Kenyon's junkyard.

"Well, well," Mr. Kenyon shouted as we pushed our bikes into his scrapyard. "What have we here, Chad? Have you brought me a little gold for recycling?" And he didn't mean the tiger—he was pointing a greasy finger at Penny's golden-brown hair.

"This is my friend Penny," I said to Mr. Kenyon.

"Pleased to meet you, Penny." He offered his hand to her as a joke. I'd seen him do it before. His hands were always black with junkyard grease and grime. He didn't really think that anyone with clean hands would shake with him.

Penny fooled him. She took his hand and gave it a good squeeze like the preacher does after church on Sundays. She didn't look at her own hand afterward, either, to see if his grime had rubbed off. "Well, aren't you sumpthin'," Mr. Kenyon said, with the broadest smile I'd ever seen on him. Penny grinned back up at him. He towered over Penny like the huge troll who stares down at the little princess in a fairy tale. He was wearing his usual black baseball cap and a pair of red suspenders that ran over his shoulders, swirled around his large belly, and ended up buttoned to his blue jeans.

He also wore a navy-blue sweatshirt with his personal advertisement printed on it: IRONMAN KENYON METAL SALVAGE. Cash for your JUNK.

"We're taking over this stretch of road, Mr. Kenyon." I pointed at the blue sign. "For the Adopt-a-Highway program. Mom and Penny and I are."

"Good," he said. "I'll see more of you then. Both of you." He smiled at Penny.

"And, another thing," I added. "Penny and I found a tiger in your ditch last night and we want you to take a look at it."

Mr. Kenyon seemed puzzled until he saw the metal tiger. "Oh, it's metal." He chuckled. "I was hoping it wouldn't bite."

"We just want to know what kind of metal it is—and how much it's worth. We think it might be brass."

While Mr. Kenyon turned the metal tiger over in his hands, I said, "I was also wondering if you had any bicycle wheels out here that I could make a bike trailer out of."

"Sure," he said, "dozens of 'em. You two just leave your fancy bikes right here where I can watch 'em, then take that road right there." He pointed at a dirt trail that wound between a mountain of old stoves, refrigerators, and washing machines on one side, and old farm equipment on the other. "Take the first turn to the left, then the next right. There's a pile of bicycles out there."

"Thanks," I said.

"Meanwhile," he said, holding up our tiger, "I'll have a better look at Mr. Tiger here."

About fifteen minutes later, we came back, each of us dragging two bikes from the pile. Mr. Kenyon was sitting on a small oil drum. The tiger stood on top of a larger oil drum. He stared at it for a moment, then, holding it with one hand and using a small wire-cutting snippers, he clipped a tiny wedge of metal out of the inside of our tiger's neck.

Penny and I watched as he took a small coin purse out of his pocket and dropped the piece of metal into it. "Those'll work," Mr. Kenyon said, looking at the bikes we had dragged up. "Choose two good front wheels and two straight front forks." He turned and pointed in a different direction. "That aluminum bakery tray over there would work for a bottom," he said, then he pointed in another direction. "And those refrigerator racks there for the sides. You can have 'em to make your trailer."

"Thanks!" I could see it already. "Perfect. But how do I fasten it all together?"

"Some of it will have to be welded," he said. "I could do that for you. For thirty years I've been cutting things apart with a welder. Welding things *together* I'm not so good at, especially fancy stuff like bikes. I'll try, though—but not until the end of next week. I have about eight truckloads of scrap to run to the city starting Monday."

"We better start cleaning the road ditches now," I said to Penny.

"Why don't you leave the tiger here with me," Mr. Kenyon said. "I'm not sure what the metal is, and I want to find out. It might be worth more than brass. Meantime, I have a good place to keep it for you."

"Sure," I said. I'd be happy with whatever we could get for the tiger. Without a head, it wasn't worth much to anybody.

Before we left, Penny turned, stuck out her hand, and said, "Pleased to meet you, Mr. Kenyon." He looked up, surprised, and stood up so quickly he knocked over the oil drum he was sitting on. It banged into a stack of scrap behind him, making a terrible clang and clatter. Mr. Kenyon smiled broadly, took Penny's hand, and shook it as gently as if it were blown glass. Then he tipped his old Chicago Cubs baseball cap to both of us as we walked our bikes out of the yard and headed up the road.

Finders, Keepers

Penny and I hadn't been gone from Ironman Kenyon's place for two minutes when she pointed up the road and hissed, "Look!"

A black Mercedes was parked on the side of the road right where we had found the tiger.

We pulled our bikes over and watched. The rear passenger door was standing open and a big man was walking in circles in the ditch, kicking the grass and hunting around. The car had dark-tinted windows. It sure looked like the same Mercedes to me.

"Is he looking for the tiger?" Penny asked in a whisper.

"Why would he?" I said. "They threw the tiger out. It didn't just *fall* out of the car—they tossed it! That makes it trash. So why would they come back to look for it now?"

Penny shook her head. "What else would they be looking for? Maybe we should we give it to him."

"But *why?* It's trash! It's finders-keepers with trash. That makes the tiger ours." Penny looked at with a weird look on her face, and I knew why. My argument was stupid. This finders-keepers thing was just an excuse because I didn't want to give up the tiger.

"If we're not going to give the tiger back," she said, "then I think we better hide. Maybe he saw us in the ditch last night. I don't want him to see us again. That guy gives me the creeps."

We pushed our bikes into a clump of bushes and watched the Mercedes from there. We knew there was somebody in the driver's seat because he threw a cigarette out the open door and into the ditch, but he never got out. The highway was dead quiet. No one came by at all.

When the big man had kicked and poked and looked for a few minutes, he walked back to the car and seemed to be talking to the person in the driver's seat. They were too far away for us to hear anything. *They* must have heard *something*, though, because all of a sudden the big man pointed up the road toward us. Penny and I both ducked down when he pointed. *He couldn't have heard us,* I thought. *We were barely whispering.*

As soon as I thought that, we heard the sound of a car coming down the highway from behind us. That must have been what he was pointing at—obviously, he didn't want to be seen in the ditch. He jumped into the Mercedes, and they zipped past us and off down the highway. Even as they passed by so close to us, I couldn't see inside the car because of the tinted windows.

When we were sure they were gone, Penny said, "I wonder if they'll be back."

"Hope not," I answered. "We should get one side of the road cleaned today. We only have 'til tomorrow to do it all."

"Let's do this side first, where we found the tiger," Penny said. "Maybe those men left something else behind."

I grinned. Those guys might give her the creeps, but she still couldn't resist an adventure.

We started right where we stood, working as fast as we could, picking up everything we could find. There was a *lot* of paper and trash—you wouldn't believe how much. We found two disposable diapers, but they'd been in the ditch so long they weren't smelly anymore. "People are really messy," I shouted, holding up a diaper by the very tip of its corner.

"They sure are," Penny shouted back, laughing and holding up an old pair of pants she had pulled out of the mud.

As we worked, we sorted cans and bottles into separate bags, trash into another. When we found something made of metal, we set it up on the roadside to give to Ironman Kenyon.

"I really like Mr. Kenyon," Penny said as she dragged a car muffler up the bank and laid it out for him.

"He likes you, too," I said.

"I think you're right," Penny said, smiling. "But if I saw him on the street, though, and didn't know him," her voice went down to a whisper, "he'd scare me shivery."

"He is pretty big," I agreed.

"And tough looking," she added.

By the middle of the morning we had cleaned to the area where we'd found the tiger and where the man had been hunting. As we picked up trash, Penny said, "Look at this."

I walked over and took a look. "It's just a cigarette butt," I said.

"But look at the writing on it," she said, holding it up under my nose.

It smelled terrible, which meant it had been smoked recently. I held my breath and studied the butt. There was strange writing on it, the same kind of writing we saw on the newspapers.

"I think this was the cigarette the Mercedes driver was smoking," Penny said. "Remember?"

"Hey—I'll take this to church with me on Sunday, too, to show the missionaries. Along with the newspapers," I said. I hunted around until I found an empty cigarette package in the grass. I slipped the foreign cigarette into it and put the package into my jacket pocket.

We worked hard until noon. By then we had cleaned more than two-thirds of the way down one side of the ditch. "Let's keep going," I said. "If we work fast for another hour or so, we can finish this side and we won't have to come back today."

We were done by 1:15. I was really sorry I didn't have a bike trailer. We could have taken most of the recyclables back to my garage with us. Instead, we hid the bags of recyclables behind some bushes so we could pick them up the next morning. Then we tied the bags of trash shut and left them up on the edge of the road, just like we'd been told in the Highway Department instructions.

Back in town, just three blocks from my house, I saw the Mercedes again. It was just a block away from us and seemed to be slowing down. I wondered if they were watching us.

The next morning, after church, I asked several older people about the newspaper. Gunda Hennum, a missionary's widow, stared at the newspaper for a long time, then looked up at me. "It's written in Pakistani," she said. She pointed to the letters across the top of the page. "It was printed in Karachi, a year ago last spring. That's the date there, see?" She pointed to the upper right-hand corner of the page. It did look something like a date, numbers and all.

A few minutes later I sat in Sunday school class trying extra hard to concentrate. I tried to put the tiger and the Pakistani newspaper out of my mind, but it kept popping back in and keeping me from listening. But then one of the kids in our class started talking about Earthkeepers, and I paid attention after that.

I told Mom about it over lunch. "How was your class, Chad?" she asked, after we had prayed over our soup and sandwiches.

"Pretty good. We got talking about God's creation—about how the earth is God's, and we're supposed to be good stewards of it. We read the creation story out of Genesis, and a couple of psalms. Most of the kids in my class are Earthkeepers members at their schools," I said.

"I'm really glad, Chad. Christians haven't always taken such good care of God's earth. You and the rest of the Earthkeepers are off to a great start. And speaking of keeping the earth, should we run out on the highway right after we eat and pick up those recyclables you said you hid in the bushes?"

"Sure."

I took another bite of sandwich and looked past Mom at the refrigerator door with all its magnets. She had fastened a MADD bumper sticker there with a magnet. That reminded me of all the different bumper stickers I had seen as I walked through the church parking lot—stickers for everything you could think of. Some of them made jokes about tailgating drivers, and some had serious messages from groups like MADD.

"We should have Earthkeepers bumper stickers," I said to Mom between spoonfuls of soup.

"Yes, we should," she agreed. "I'd put one on my car."

"Who makes stickers anyway?" I asked.

"I suppose you could have bumper stickers printed in lots of places—but first you'd need someone to design it. Tomorrow I'll give Judy Seleen a call. She does design work for our church headquarters. Maybe she'd put one together for you in her spare time."

We cleaned up the kitchen. As we got into the car to go out and pick up the bags of cans and bottles, Mom asked, "Should we pick up Penny?"

"They're gone until this afternoon," I said. "Besides, there are only a few bags of bottles and cans. You won't even have to get out of the car."

Or at least, that's what I thought. But when we got near enough to our stretch of highway that we could read the "Adopt-a-Highway" sign, I saw something strange. I leaned forward and stared, thinking my eyes were playing tricks. But Mom had seen it, too.

"Look at that," she said. "I thought you and Penny had finished cleaning up yesterday. Weren't you supposed to put that stuff in bags?"

"We *did.*"

"Well, just look at that," Mom said. She pulled over and popped the button to turn on the emergency flashers.

We walked to the front of the car. The garbage bag that Penny and I had so carefully filled had been ripped open and dumped on the roadside. It looked like someone had kicked through it, like I might kick through a pile of leaves in the fall.

I looked up from the mess and let my eyes focus down along the road. There was a trail of torn-open trash bags from where we stood all the way down the right side of the highway. It stretched almost to Mr. Kenyon's junkyard. Every few hundred feet, the bags we had filled and laid so carefully along the edge of the highway had been opened and the trash scattered around.

But why? Did somebody do this to get even with Penny and me for something? No, of course not. Penny and I didn't have any enemies—not really. Teasers, maybe, but not enemies. Besides, only Mom and Mr. Kenyon knew we'd been out here.

"Who'd have done such a thing?" Mom asked. "Would your friend, Mr. Kenyon, have gone through these bags looking for scrap?"

"Oh, Mom." I rolled my eyes. "Come on."

"Well, would he?"

"If he had, he wouldn't have left a mess—any more than I would have. Besides, he knew Penny and I were doing the cleaning."

"What does that mean?"

"That means he knew that anyone from Earth-keepers would already have separated out the recyclables."

Mom pushed some of the trash with her toe. "Maybe it was just kids," she said. "You know, vandalism." But then she shook her head. "No, kids wouldn't walk two miles along a highway just to make a mess. Kids usually smash up something they're angry with—a school, or a store, or somebody's house."

"You know what bugs me about this?" I said. "You try to do something good, and something like this happens. It's not fair."

"Well—too bad we don't have trash bags with us, we could clean up right now." Mom stopped then and hit her forehead with the heel of her hand. "Oh, Chad. I forgot. I'm showing the Herkenroth house again this afternoon. We'll have to clean this up tomorrow morning before work."

"I'm going to hate picking up all this stuff a second time," I said. "Makes me mad."

When we got home, I began to think of the mess along the highway and of how busy Mom was these days. I knew she had to sell houses, but sometimes I missed having her around—even just to do something disgusting like cleaning up a mess.

In this case, a *big* mess. And out along a stretch of highway that Mom and Penny and I were supposed to keep clean. Penny was gone for the day—I couldn't ask her to help. I could call Jay. He might do it. But he'd grumble the whole time. I sighed, took a box of trash bags, and biked out to the highway to clean up—all by myself.

It didn't take nearly as long to rebag the trash as it had taken to pick it up in the first place. But working without Penny, and having to redo what I'd already done once, was no fun. I asked myself a dozen times as I worked along the roadside, "Who made this mess—and why?"

The Trailer

When Mom came home later that night, I was working furiously over a yellow scratch pad, scribbling designs for my bike trailer. I had it pretty well figured out. I'd use the 20-inch wheels Penny and I had found at Mr. Kenyon's, set them about two feet apart, and mount the aluminum tray in between.

Mom looked over my shoulder at the drawings, then snapped her fingers as she sometimes does when she has just remembered something. I was just about to ask her what it was when she started asking my a lot of questions about my drawings—pointing things out, asking how I was going to use the trailer, how big it had to be, what I would make it out of. Finally, she asked if a kiddie trailer like we had talked about could be remodeled into a junk trailer.

"Sure," I said. "Easy."

"That's interesting, because on the way to work on Friday, I spotted one of those kiddie trailers next to a garbage can across town."

"Really?"

"Really. It looked like someone had backed over it with a car."

"Oh, wow. I wonder if it could be fixed. How bad was it?"

"Pretty bad."

"Would it still be there?"

"When I saw it, the garbage truck was only a half-block away. It would have been picked up in just a few minutes."

"Oh," I moaned. "Too bad."

She grinned. "I didn't say the garbage truck *got* it. I said the garbage truck was a half-block away."

"What happened to it then?"

"It's out in the trunk of my car," Mom said, digging in her purse, then holding up the car keys like a trophy. "It's been in there since Friday. I forgot all about it until I saw your drawing."

"All right! Mom, you're great," I said, giving her a big hug and a smack on the cheek. "Not many moms would stop at the curb and pick up someone's junk."

She rubbed the cheek where I had kissed her. "For a kiss like that, I'll bring home junk for you every day."

I ran outside, wondering how she could have forgotten something so important. I quickly swung open the trunk, and there it sat—a crippled little trailer. The yellow plastic double seat was cracked and twisted in several places. Someone had really done a job on it. I didn't care about the seat, though. I just wanted the frame.

But it was twisted, too. One wheel was fine, but the other one was bent into a shallow U-shape. It looked pretty bad. I didn't know whether I could fix it.

I lifted the trailer out of the trunk, closed the lid, and carried it into the garage. I ran Mom's keys back in to her, just nodding when she asked, "It's pretty bad, isn't it?"

I was dragging the trailer to the middle of the garage floor when Penny came in. "Your mom said you were out here. She told me about the mess out on the highway. Did you clean it up all by yourself?"

"Yeah," I said. "What a stupid deal."

"Why would anyone do that?" Penny asked.

"Don't ask me."

Penny looked at the little trailer from a couple of angles and said, "It's really wrecked." She shook her head. "Looks hopeless."

"I don't think so."

"You can't possibly fix that."

"It just has to be good enough so we could go out and get our recyclables. Give me a hand."

"Doing what?"

"Straightening the wheel, for one thing."

I slid two cement blocks out of the corner of the garage, took the tire and tube off the wheel, then laid the wheel across the cement blocks like a little bridge.

"Now we have to jump on it," I said.

"Both of us?"

"I think so."

"Why don't you just buy a new wheel?" Penny asked.

"Easy for you to say." That was the way Penny's family solved most of their problems—by buying more things and spending more money. When Penny bent her bike wheel in the race last summer, she just rode my bike downtown and bought a new one—or more likely, she charged a new one to her dad. Mom doesn't have the money for that. Besides, that isn't the Earthkeepers way. In Earthkeepers, we learn to recycle. "We just saved three wheels like this out at Ironman's," I said. "He gave them to us. Why buy what we can get free? Besides, what we don't buy doesn't end up in a landfill."

Penny sighed. "I forgot. That's kind of an Earth-keepers rule, isn't it: Recycle, don't replace."

"Right," I grinned.

"But we can't get Mr. Kenyon's wheels until Monday after school," Penny said.

"I know. That's why we're straightening *this* wheel. We need it just for right now. Want to ride out with me and get the recyclables?"

"Sure," Penny said.

We had a few laughs jumping on the wheel to straighten it. It was tricky keeping our balance, and we fell a few times, the wheel rolling and clattering around the garage.

When we had straightened the wheel as much as we could, Penny helped me pound the little trailer frame until it was straighter. Then I put on the tire, pumped it up, and put everything back together.

"I think it'll work now," I said, pulling the trailer around in a little circle on the garage floor. It thumped and hopped on the partly straightened wheel, but it worked. "Toss me that roll of duct tape," I said. "We can use it to fix the seat."

We peeled strips off the roll of gray tape and taped the shattered plastic seat back together. When we were through, we stepped back to look. "I wouldn't put a baby in it," Penny said, "but it's good enough for hauling junk."

"Chad and Penny's Trailer Repair Service," I said in a TV announcer's voice.

"Let's go before it gets dark," Penny said, ducking down so she could see the sky out of the garage windows.

We biked to our section of road, slipped our orange vests over our jackets, and stood there trying to decide what to do first. "Since we're so close," Penny said, "lets run the scrap metal out first. We can leave it at Mr. Kenyon's gate. Then let's load up the recycling bags and haul them back to your garage before it gets dark. We'll have to hurry."

We rode along the edge of the road, stopping now and then to pick up the metal objects we had laid along the roadside the day before. Soon my little trailer looked like a porcupine—a car muffler, an exhaust pipe, a tangle of wire, and several other metal objects stuck out in every direction.

We rode up to Ironman's gate and tossed the junk into a pile next to his gate, where I was sure he'd find it the next morning. We pedaled back along the road until we came to the bushes we had hidden our recyclables behind.

"Look at that," Penny said.

The recycling bags were dumped and emptied, too, just like the ones had been up on the road.

We had to rebag everything. Finally, we dragged two bags of bottles and two bags of cans across the ditch and up to the trailer. "I can carry one of these bags of aluminum cans on my handlebars," Penny said. "They don't weigh very much."

"That's why they make airplanes out of them."

Penny laughed. "Well, next time I fly, I hope the plane's made out of something sturdier than aluminum cans." She slapped the bag, making it rattle.

"Ha ha. You know what I meant."

We stacked the two bags of bottles in the little trailer, filling it, and I put the other sack of aluminum cans across my handlebars. The sun was setting as we started off down the road for home, and I remembered the warnings from the State Department of Transportation about not working along the road when visibility is poor or when there is too much traffic.

"We'd better move it," I said. "It's getting dark."

"We still have half the road to clean up, remember," Penny said. "We'll have to come out here tomorrow after school."

"Maybe we can get some other kids to help us. Jay, maybe, and Pedro."

We could see a car's headlights coming toward us, and as it got close I recognized it—the black Mercedes. It slowed down as it went by. I couldn't see inside the car, but I had the feeling that whoever was inside was staring at us. They could hardly miss us in our blaze-orange vests with reflecting tape.

It sped up again after it had passed us. I shuddered and said to Penny, "You're right—those guys give me the creeps, too."

I looked over my shoulder. The Mercedes had stopped and backed into the driveway at Ironman Kenyon's junkyard. "It's turning around," I called. "It's coming our way."

"Let's get off the road," she shouted back. "Let's hide."

"Where?" I asked. There weren't any bushes to hide behind on this part of the road.

"In that farmyard." Penny dug hard at her pedals and zoomed away.

We both pumped our bikes as hard as we could, my little trailer thumped badly behind me. When we turned into the farm driveway, we were going as fast as we dared, fast enough to slide on the gravel. The trailer skidded around the corner and tipped up on one wheel. The bottles in the bags clinked and jangled, but they stayed in the trailer.

"Behind that pickup truck," Penny shouted. We steered our bikes behind an old pickup truck parked in the farmyard. We jumped off the bikes and leaned them against the truck. No one in sight, no lights in either the house or in the barn. A horse whinnied somewhere, but otherwise the farm was silent. The people who lived there were probably gone for the day. I'd have felt better, I think, if there'd been someone home. If the Mercedes drove in and found us, there was no one to help.

We didn't dare peek around the truck, so I flopped on the ground and looked under it. Penny flopped down beside me. We lay there staring at the

road until the Mercedes pulled to a stop at the end of the driveway. There was no sound except the soft idling of the engine. No one got out. They just parked there for a minute or two. Then they drove off. The horse whinnied again, and then everything was quiet.

"They're after us," Penny said. "They think we have the tiger."

"Yeah, I think you're right," I said. "But we don't have the tiger. Mr. Kenyon has it."

We waited for several minutes, then I walked out to the end of the driveway and looked both ways. The road was deserted.

"Let's get home," Penny said.

We didn't waste any time. I thought I could see a black Mercedes lurking in every shadow on the way home.

The Tiger Hunt

The highway department agreed to give us a couple more days to clean up the road. Mom said she would plan to leave the office early on Tuesday and help.

So on Monday after school, Penny and I rode out to Kenyon's junkyard, the trailer wobbling and bouncing along behind my bike. "Did you find the little pile of scrap we left at your gate?" I called to Mr. Kenyon as we climbed off our bikes.

"Which one?" he smiled, lumbering toward us. "There were four piles here this morning. Someone left that old refrigerator, too." He pointed at it. "I should have a weekend every other day. People give me free scrap on weekends."

"Our pile had a car muffler in it, and some wire, and other pieces of metal I didn't recognize," I said.

"Oh. You had a chunk of power take-off shaft from a tractor," Mr. Kenyon explained, "a skid from one of the county's road graders, and the tin cover to a lawnmower engine. Where'd you get that stuff?"

"Right down the road there," Penny said, pointing, "while we were cleaning the ditch. The same side we found the tiger on."

"I still haven't figured out that metal," Mr. Kenyon said. We knew he meant the tiger. "I did study it a bit, though. It's a heavy little thing. You'd think she'd be solid instead of hollow, being that heavy. More like lead than brass. But she's yellow metal, sure enough. You shine her up, she might be real pretty on a shelf—if she still had her head."

"That's exactly what I said." Penny smiled.

"She's a softer color than brass, and a softer metal, too. If she were a little more silver colored, I'd think she had lead in her. I got to thinking it might be—well, no point in dreaming."

"What does that mean?" Penny asked him.

"Oh, nothing. I'm just babbling." Mr. Kenyon winked at us. "Come on, let's weigh her up."

We followed him into his office shed. On top of his filing cabinet, on every shelf, and piled high on his desk were little treasures he had saved out of people's junk. Brass ashtrays, light fixtures, bowling trophies, toys, tools. On the wall above his desk hung a few pieces of junk he had welded together to look like a roadrunner bird.

In the corner of the office was a huge old iron safe. He turned the dial twice and swung it open. It was full, too. He reached in and pulled out the tiger. "You keep it in a safe?" Penny asked, surprised.

"I never want to lose anything that doesn't belong to me," he replied.

We walked back out of the office and over to his platform scale. He bent over, pulled a dirty cloth glove out of his back pocket, and brushed off the scale's dented and scratched metal platform with the glove. Then he set the tiger down on its feet. "Don't want her to stand in all that dirt," he said with a wink.

Slowly and carefully he shifted the weights on the scale's dull brass balance bar, finally tapping the smaller weight with the tip of his finger. When the pointer rested exactly in the middle of the opening at the end, he bent over to read the numbers. "Nine pounds, twelve and a half—no, two-thirds ounces," he said. "Nine pounds, twelve point six ounces."

"How much is that worth if it's brass?" Penny asked.

"Well, Penny, you see there's yellow brass and there's red brass. Some people call red brass bronze. Bronze has copper in it and sometimes tin. Right now I'm paying forty-five cents a pound for yellow brass and sixty-five cents a pound for red brass. If that's yellow brass—which I'm not sure it is, ten pounds of it is worth about four dollars and fifty cents."

"I wish we could find its head," I said. "It might be worth more then, as a statue."

"Well, don't sell it yet," Mr. Kenyon said. "Let me check on the metal for you. I'll take that little piece I snipped off to the city. I can let you know in a day or two." He picked up the tiger again, held it in front of him and asked, "Should I put her back in the safe?"

"Naw," I said. "We'll take her home with us."

"Put her in a safe place, then," he said. "I mean, in case you find her head."

I wrapped the tiger loosely in its canvas and set it in my trailer.

"Where did you get that bent-up trailer?" Mr. Kenyon asked.

"My mom picked it out of someone's trash. Look at this wheel, Mr. Kenyon." I pointed, lifting one side of the trailer and spinning the wheel.

"She's a wobbler, all right."

"Do you suppose I could use one of those wheels we pulled out of the pile?" I asked, pointing to the bike frames we had dragged up, still lying where we had left them.

"I said you could have them and you can," he said, pulling a long pair of battery pliers out of his pocket and walking over to the bicycles. He spun the two front wheels, unbolted the best of the two, and handed it to me.

Five minutes later Penny and I rode back into town with the small wheel and the headless tiger in my trailer. Penny rode back to her house for dinner.

When I walked into the kitchen, Mom set down the pan she was holding and said, "You won't believe what happened."

"What?" I asked.

"You remember I told you that the Herkenroths were moving?"

"Sure."

"They were almost all packed, everything was in boxes. Someone got into their house on Saturday night and ripped open every single box. Things were strewn everywhere. I had to postpone the showing."

"Wow," I said. "Did they steal anything?"

"The police weren't sure, everything was such a mess. Things were broken, but so far the Herkenroths haven't found anything was missing."

I walked back out to the garage thinking of the mess along the highway and of the mess someone had made of Herkenroth's packed boxes. I stood for a long time staring at my trailer with the cloth-wrapped tiger in it. There was one thing I was sure of, for some reason: The messes were related.

Whoever threw out the tiger wanted it back—and bad. They'd searched through the bags on the highway, and when they hadn't found it there, they'd seen the Herkenroth's name on the Adopt-a-Highway signs, found their house, broken in, and searched through their things, too. They'd probably figured that the two kids on bikes were Herkenroths.

I picked up the tiger, surprised once again at how heavy it was for its size, and carried it back to the workbench. "Why are those men in the Mercedes hunting for this tiger?" I asked myself in a whisper, "and why would they want it back after they tossed it out like trash?"

Mr. Kenyon's words came back to me: "*Put her in a safe place.*"

But where? In the garage? In the house? At Penny's house?

I looked around the garage for a hiding place. Nothing except maybe for the big box of aluminum cans over in the corner. That box came to my rescue once before, when Penny and I helped break up a stolen-gun ring last summer. Maybe it would help me again.

I kneeled in front of the box and set the tiger on the floor, then dug a hole in the cans. I tucked the tiger into the hole and covered it with aluminum cans.

I thought back to Friday evening, and the flying tiger that almost hit Penny in the nose, and the Mercedes—and the police car right behind it.

Maybe the police are already on these guys' case, I thought. *Maybe that's why they were tailing them that night. On the other hand, they haven't broken any laws yet—at least not that I've got proof of. If these guys are dangerous, though, Penny and I could be in big trouble. So do I call the police?* I thought it over for a minute. "Not until I'm more sure," I answered myself in a whisper.

Meanwhile—finders, keepers.

The Body Is Lost

I went out to the garage before school on Tuesday morning to check on the tiger. I dug it out of the box of cans and set it on the workbench. *What is it about this tiger,* I thought, *that would drive someone to rummage through a bunch of smelly, yucky trash bags—and then risk breaking into a house?*

I stared at it for a minute, and then I picked it up. It was really neat. It looked like the tigers you see in old movies about Egypt. I carried it over to the window and stared down through the hole in the neck into the hollow inside. *In a detective movie,* I thought, *there'd be a secret compartment inside with a diamond in it worth a million dollars.* My hand wouldn't quite fit inside. But my hands were pretty big—bigger than most of the guys' at school. Mom's hand probably would fit, or Penny's. I felt inside as far as I could with my fingers. Was something hidden in there? Was this tiger stuffed with drugs or money—or had it been? Was that why someone had taken the head off? To get at what was inside?

Sounds pretty crazy, I thought. *This isn't a movie.* But still, this headless tiger was pretty important to someone, and I wanted to know why.

Just then Jay walked in. "Whatcha doin'?" he asked.

"Look at this." I handed it to him.

"Wow! It's really heavy. Where'd you get it?"

"Penny and I found it while we were cleaning the highway." I told him about the Adopt-a-Highway program.

"Too bad the head's gone," Jay mumbled, studying the tiger closely. "We're doing plaster casting in art class—I'd love to do a casting of this."

"Probably isn't worth anything without the head," I said. I rewrapped the headless tiger. Jay watched as I reburied it under the aluminum cans.

"If it isn't worth anything, why are you hiding it?" he asked.

"I think the people who threw it away want it back."

"So why not just give it to them?"

Actually, there was a good answer to that question. If these guys *were* the same ones who broke into the Herkenroths' house, then they could be dangerous. Still, I could take it to the police and let them decide what to do with it. Why *didn't* I? Maybe I wanted to keep it. Or maybe I just didn't want to give it to people who acted as creepy as those guys in the Mercedes acted. But the truth was probably something I learned about myself back when Penny and I found that gun in the garbage—I don't like to turn loose of an adventure once I've found one. Even a scary one.

"We better get to school," I said, changing the subject. "Hey—want to help Penny and me clean the highway this afternoon?"

"Can't," he said as we hopped on our bikes and started down the alley. "I have to stay after school. My art project is due tomorrow."

After school, Pedro, Penny, Mom, and I went out to the highway to finish cleaning up. Mom and Pedro had gotten to be friends when Mom helped his family find a place to live last year. Mom and Pedro worked out of the car. Penny and I rode our bikes. I pulled the trailer to haul any metal we found.

We worked fast—the four of us finished the other side in a little over an hour. Mom put all the recyclables in her trunk and drove off to take Pedro home. Penny and I biked toward Mr. Kenyon's yard with a load of scrap in my trailer.

"No more tigers, eh?" Mr. Kenyon asked as he and Penny and I unloaded our trailer.

"Nope," Penny said.

"Where did you put your headless tiger?"

"At home in my garage," I said, "hidden in a box of aluminum cans."

"Box of cans? Hmmm," Mr. Kenyon said. "I think you ought to put it in a safer place."

"Why?" Penny asked. "Did you have that piece of metal examined? Is it some super-special kind of brass?"

"Well, it isn't exactly brass, but I'd be willing to pay you red-brass price for it—maybe even a little more. Let's see, if we rounded it off to ten pounds, red brass is selling for sixty-five cents, that would make the little critter worth about six dollars and fifty cents—that is, if it were red brass. So—would you take ten dollars for it?" Mr. Kenyon had a funny smile on his face.

"Sure—I guess," I answered.

"What about a hundred dollars? Or a thousand?"

A thousand dollars? For a few seconds, neither Penny nor I could say anything. "You're joking, right?" Penny asked finally.

Ironman Kenyon started to laugh. The laugh sounded like it started down around his knees and then rolled up through him like a volcano. "Well, to tell you the truth," he said with another laugh, "I would be happy to pay that for it—and a lot more if I had to. That's why you shouldn't be keeping it in your garage."

"What do you mean?" I asked.

"I mean that little tiger isn't brass. It's gold."

"Gold?" Penny and I said together.

"It's really gold?" I asked.

"It's not only gold, the people at the Mines and Minerals Office said it's very *old* gold. Just that little piece I pinched off is worth about fifty dollars."

"Wow," Penny breathed.

"Wow," I echoed.

"That's why they painted it black. So no one would suspect it's gold. So how much is the tiger worth?"

"I wondered that, too," Mr. Kenyon said, "so I looked in the paper this morning. The price of gold goes up and down because rich people and governments buy and sell it. This morning, gold was selling at about four hundred dollars an ounce. Tomorrow it could be three hundred—or six hundred. There are twelve troy ounces in a pound."

"What's a troy ounce?"

"It's a special way jewelers weigh gold and silver."

"So how much is ten pounds worth?" I asked anxiously.

"I'd better write that out so I get the right number of zeros," Mr. Kenyon said. He took a pencil stub out of his breast pocket and scribbled some numbers on the hood of a beat-up old pickup truck.

"Ten pounds is one hundred-twenty troy ounces," he mumbled as he worked. "At four hundred dollars each that's —" He multiplied the numbers. The pencil clicked against the painted metal. "Whew," he said.

"How *much?*" I asked.

"Today, that ten pounds of gold would be worth about $48,000."

Neither of us said anything. What can you say when somebody tells you you've got something sitting in your garage worth $48,000?

"But of course no one would sell that little tiger for scrap gold, even to get $48,000," Mr. Kenyon added, "because it's very old. The people at the minerals office said the little critter was cast over three thousand years ago.

"Wow!" I said. "Before Jesus was even born."

"Yup. Which means that's a pretty important little hunk of metal. They asked me a lot of questions, wondering how somebody like me got hold of something like that. They almost called the police—and I think that's what *you* should do. Who knows where this thing came from—or where it ought to be."

"Three thousand years ago means it came from somewhere far away," Penny said, "maybe from Egypt."

"Or Pakistan," I said to Penny, "like the paper."

"Paper?" Mr. Kenyon asked.

"Newspaper. When we found it," Penny said, "it was wrapped in a Pakistani newspaper."

"I think you two had better scoot home," Mr. Kenyon whispered. "Call the police, and then get that little tiger into a bank vault."

"The banks are already closed," Penny said.

"Then you'd better find a safer place to hide it than a box of cans," he said. He reached into his shirt pocket and took out a sealed white envelope. "This is the little piece I pinched off."

Just as I was about to tell Mr. Kenyon he could keep it, the truth hit me—this wasn't my gold to give away. Finding a hunk of brass worth less than five dollars was one thing. Ten pounds of gold worth $48,000 was another. Now we *had* to call the police—the minute we got home!

Penny and I rode back to my garage so fast we didn't even talk as we pedaled. When we got there we pushed our bikes inside and leaned them against the wall, and I ran to the aluminum can box. I reached into the middle, where I had buried the tiger, then swirled my hand around among the cans, clinking them against each other, trying to find that heavy bundle of cloth. When I didn't feel it, I began to move my hand around faster and faster, in larger and larger circles. Then I dropped to my knees and thrashed around in the box

with both hands like a crazy person. Finally I lifted the box and shook it hard.

"What's wrong?" Penny asked.

I turned the box upside down and dumped all the cans on the floor. "It's gone!" I gasped. "The tiger's gone!"

But the Head Is Found

"Where could it have gone?" Penny asked, turning around, her eyes darting from place to place. "Did you put it somewhere else? Could you have moved it?""

"I would have remembered!" I hissed, angry and frustrated. "Someone stole it. It was right in there," I said, pointing at the box and the pile of cans strewn around the floor.

"Who knew about it?" Penny asked, stooping to pick up cans and throw them back in the box.

"You and I," I started to count on my fingers, "and Mr. Kenyon, and Mom—and I showed it to Jay."

"Would Jay have taken it?" Penny asked, looking up. "He talked about some art project, but if he wanted to borrow it, he'd have asked."

"You told Mr. Kenyon exactly where the tiger was, didn't you?" asked Penny.

"Yeah," I answered. "So?"

"So maybe he jumped in his pickup truck, drove here ahead of us, and took it." She dumped an armload of cans into the box.

"Look," I said, picking up a can myself and throwing it in, "if he'd wanted to steal it, he could have bought the gold tiger for four dollars and fifty cents. I'd have sold it, thinking it was brass."

"I guess so." Penny sighed. "Besides, Mr. Kenyon's too nice to steal."

"But *someone* took it."

"Well, let's call the police," Penny said. "If it's really that old, it was probably stolen from a museum somewhere. We could get in trouble."

"We could get in trouble if we *do* call. What would we say? We don't even *have* the tiger. If it *was* stolen, they might think we've still got it and we're just hiding it somewhere." I was starting to get really worried. What if somebody blamed *us* for losing something worth $48,000? Even if we put together what I earned each week selling scrap, and added Penny's allowance, it would take us a hundred years to pay it back.

"The problem is," I finally said, sinking down on a cold cement block, "that the tiger was never ours in the first place. It was way too valuable to be 'finders, keepers.'"

"Well, we didn't know that when we found it," Penny sighed, sinking down near me on another concrete block. "So what do we do now—just forget about it? Just let whoever has it now keep it?"

"But we don't know who has it! What if *they* don't own it? That tiger's valuable, and I'm sure whoever *really* owns it wants it back."

"Well, someone sure wants it back, owner or not," Penny said. "Someone wanted it bad enough to break into the Herkenroths' house. That was a crime. And maybe littering the highway with our trash was a crime, too."

"We have to do *something*," I said. "Maybe we should ride around town and look for the black Mercedes."

Penny thought that over, nodded, and then stood up. "But what do we do if we find the Mercedes?" she asked.

"Watch," I suggested, "and see if anyone does anything suspicious."

"Where would we look for a car like that?"

"Maybe down at the Riverside Hotel."

"Good thinking," Penny said. "That's where we'll start. Just let me put this little chunk of gold someplace safe," I said, pulling the envelope from my pocket. "Then we'll go."

When we got downtown we rode along the street in front of the Riverside Hotel, checking the cars parked there. Then we rode through the alley and checked out the parking lot in the back by the river. No black Mercedes there, either.

"It's getting dark," Penny said, "and we don't have lights."

Just as we were about to leave, the black Mercedes drove in at the end of the alley. "Yes!" Penny said when she saw the car. Before she could say anything else, I pushed her and her bike back between two parked cars, then I ducked in with my bike too. She hissed, "Shhh." I didn't have to be told.

"It's the same man we saw hunting in the ditch," Penny whispered as the big man stepped out of the Mercedes. "He's like a mountain."

He looked even bigger up close. The huge man locked the car and disappeared through the rear door of the hotel. "We'd better get out of here," Penny said.

Just as we were about to leave, another man came out of the hotel and walked to the car. He was very dark-skinned and had beautiful white teeth. He looked something like Tammy Kanavati's father. They go to our church, but originally they're from India.

Could this man be from Pakistan? I wondered. *Would that explain the newspaper and the cigarette?*

The man stood beside the Mercedes for a minute. At first I thought he was going to get into the car, but he just leaned over and looked through the driver's door window. Then, as if he had changed his mind, he stood up and walked away along the river.

Penny and I pushed our bikes out from between the parked cars, jumped on, and rode to the end of the block. We pushed our bikes across the river bridge, across the highway, and then zigzagged on sidewalks back to my garage.

"I wish we could find out who that man was," I said. "He looked like he was from India."

"I thought so, too," Penny said. "Could we ask who he was at the hotel desk?"

"They wouldn't tell us," I said. "They can't."

"Maybe we could get a name, though," Penny said.

"How?"

"By using a *wrong* name. I read it in one of my mysteries. Can you think up a name someone from India would have?"

"Kanavati, like the family at my church? No, the desk clerk might know them—that might sound suspicious."

We both thought for a minute or two and couldn't come up with any. Other than Gandhi and Kanavati, the only names we could dream up sounded more German or Dutch. "All I can think of," I finally said, "are the names of Indian cities from our geography class."

"We can't call and ask for Mr. New Delhi, can we?" Penny giggled.

"What about Ranchipur?" I asked.

"Ranchipur might work." Penny brightened. "Let's try it." We ran into our kitchen and Penny looked up the hotel number and dialed. Without even practicing, her voice transformed into a strange Indian accent. She asked, "Ees my Ohnkle, Meeester *Ranch*eepoor regeestered zehr pl*ee*ze. He eeese from *Eeen*dya." There was a long pause as Penny listened, then she said, "Yesss, he ahlzo goes by *zat* name. Thank yeeo ver*ee* mooch," and hung up.

"You were great." I patted her on the back.

"His name is Orandi." Penny grinned.

"Your Uncle Orandi." I laughed.

Penny and I sat at the kitchen table. She absent-mindedly flipped the front section of the paper toward her and began to scan the headlines in Section B. Suddenly her eyes got as big as pizzas. "Look!" she cried, pointing at the newspaper.

Pointing with her finger, she spun the newspaper around on the table so I could see. There they were, as big as life: two pictures of our tiger. One had been taken when its head was still on and before it was painted black. The other was a picture of just the head, painted black—the head that had been taken off, the mystery head that we had never seen. "There's the missing head." Penny pointed at the paper. She stood up and walked around the edge of the table so we could both read the article.

POLICE FIND HEAD OF ANCIENT SCULPTURE.

Metropolitan police have recovered the head of a priceless Mesopotamian sculpture, a tiger cast of pure gold. Until today, international police and insurance investigators have had no leads or suspects since the sculpture disappeared from a museum in Athens, Greece, over a year ago. Police and FBI agents hope that the body of the tiger is still in the area and can also be recovered.

I felt really weird. There was a picture of our tiger, right there in the paper. And police from all over the world were hunting for it. "Well, that answers some questions," I said. "That's why we should help get it back. Because it belongs to a museum."

"That's what I said in the first place," Penny reminded me. "But we don't have it any more—and we don't have a clue where it is."

We sat for a minute or two in silence, then I said softly, "Well, one good thing—now we can talk to the police."

"Right." Penny nodded. "In fact, we don't have much choice. How should we do it?"

"I think we should tell my mom first, and then the police. It's up to them what happens after that."

When Mom walked through the door a few minutes later, I said, "Mom, we've got a story for you that you won't believe," and handed her the paper.

"Well," she said, when we'd told her everything, "I think you're right—we'd better call the police, and we'd better call them right now. I just wish, Chad, that you'd told me all this as soon as you saw the connection between the vandalism on the highway and the break-in at the Herkenroths'. These people sound like dangerous criminals to me."

Mom called the police station and asked for Monty Irwin. She's friends with his wife. He's the one who helped us last summer when we found the gun in the garbage can—although, at first, we thought he was one of the bad guys. Mom was on hold for a long time, then Mr. Irwin came on. Yes, he had seen the article on the tiger and, yes, he had also noticed the black Mercedes around town. He'd come right over.

"You know," Penny said as Mom hung up, "we still don't have any proof that we ever had the tiger."

Wait a minute. "We do so have proof," I said, remembering suddenly and jumping up. "We have this." I pulled an envelope from the butter crock on top of the refrigerator.

"The little chunk of gold," Penny said, recognizing the envelope.

"They already have the head," I said. "This little piece of gold will match the gold in the head."

"But where's the body?" Penny wondered, wrinkling her forehead. "Who took it from your garage?"

Kidnapping Is FBI Business

After we'd told Monty Irwin the whole story, sitting in our living room, he still had lots of questions, and Mom had some, too. Then he spent a long time on the telephone in the kitchen, making several calls. When he was done, he sat back down on the couch and looked at us quietly. He looked worried. "Well," he said, "I called New York. We'll get mug shots of known art smugglers on the fax machine first thing tomorrow morning."

"Did you ask them about Mr. Orandi?" Penny asked.

"The only Orandi the New York office knows is the owner of an art auction house in Boston. They said they'd try to track him down, and maybe send a picture of him also."

"Maybe he's turned crook," I said.

Mr. Irwin shrugged. "Well, stranger things have happened. Although he's cooperated with the police in other investigations in the past."

"He sure scared us," Penny said with a shiver.

"What should we do now?" I asked.

"You should stay out of it," Mr. Irwin said gently. "Just go to school and be good kids."

"That's pretty hard," Penny said, "Not the good kids part," she laughed, "but staying out of it. We've had $48,000 worth of gold in our hands."

"That statue's probably worth a lot more than $48,000, considering how much trouble everybody's going to trying to find it. And that's all the more reason for you to not get involved," Mr. Irwin said. As he got up to leave, he picked up the snippet of gold in the envelope. "I'll send this to the lab," he said, sticking it into his coat pocket. "Call us if you remember anything more."

The house was quiet after he left—*as quiet as church,* I thought, and that reminded me that I hadn't prayed about any of this yet. Mom had gone into the kitchen, Penny seemed to be lost in her own thoughts, and I decided this was as good a time as any. *Help everything work out, Lord,* I prayed silently. *There are some bad people around here, and somebody could get hurt. Please protect us all. And when everything's over and everybody's safe, remind us all that you're the one who saved us. Amen.*

On the way home from school the next day, Penny and I checked the Riverside Hotel parking lot. No Mercedes.

"Well, it was here this morning," I said.

"Suppose they left town?" Penny asked as we stood straddling our bikes at the edge of the parking lot.

"Maybe," I answered with a shrug.

"I wonder if it was Mr. Orandi who threw the gold tiger out of the Mercedes."

"Either him or the mountain man," I said.

72

Suddenly Mr. Orandi stepped out of the back door of the hotel. He saw us, looked as if he recognized us and turned in our direction.

We rode off as fast as we could.

"Wait!" he shouted after us.

No way, I thought, tilting my bike around a corner. *We'll be in all kinds of trouble if we don't stay out of this.*

On Thursday just before lunch, Penny and I were both called to the principal's office. "Officer Irwin has called to ask if the two of you can be released for the afternoon," the principal said. "Apparently, he needs to question you about some police matters," he added, looking at us suspiciously.

Gosh, I thought, *I feel guilty and I haven't even done anything wrong.*

"I've already cleared things with your parents," he said, "so you're both to go right to the Buckworth's. Officer Irwin will meet you there."

When we got to my house, Monty Irwin and Mom were there—and also a man we hadn't met before, a man from Lloyds of London, an insurance company. His name was Mr. Selby.

"Tell it all again," Mr. Irwin told us. "Mr. Selby needs to hear your story. Maybe you'll think of something you left out."

We told the whole story again. Mr. Selby looked and sounded very British, and he nodded the whole time we were talking, except when he was asking questions. "Well then," he said when we were done, sitting back in his chair and looking from us to Monty Irwin, "we've gone for a year without being able to ascertain the whereabouts of this sculpture at all, and now suddenly we have the head, and the miscreants who stole it are searching for the body as hard as we are."

"Ascertain?" "Miscreants?" Boy, they sure talk funny in England. But we learned one thing for sure from listening to Mr. Selby and Officer Irwin—the guys in the black Mercedes were still in town, and they still wanted the statue.

Mr. Irwin and Mr. Selby left our house about 3:00. Too late to go back to school, but Mom went back to work. Penny and I decided to haul a load of aluminum cans out to Ironman Kenyon's. I folded up Section B of the paper and slipped it inside my coat, in case he hadn't seen it.

When we neared our section of highway, Penny pulled up her bike and said, "Look."

They had changed the "Adopt-a-Highway" signs. Now *our* names were on them: *Mrs. Claire and Chadwicke Buckworth, and Penelope Palmer*

"My name, too." Penny grinned.

"Yeah—great," I said. *Hmm.* "Or maybe not so great."

"What does that mean?" Penny asked.

"If our guess is right, somebody broke into the Herkenroths' because of those signs. Now *our* names are on there."

Penny nodded, thinking it over.

Another thought occurred to me: What would the tease guys say when they saw my name and Penny's name on the same sign? Oh well.

We delivered the bag of cans to Mr. Kenyon and told him the tiger was missing.

"I didn't think your garage was a very good hiding place," he said quietly, shaking his head.

He'd already seen the pictures in the *Metro Tribune,* and he'd tried several times to call our house, but it must have been while we were still at school.

"You two better be extra careful," he said.

Before we hopped on our bikes, Penny and I split the three dollars and sixty-five cents he gave us for the aluminum cans. We played "Paper, Scissors, and Rock," best three out of five, for the extra penny, standing outside Ironman's gate.

As we stood there, the black Mercedes drove by, slowed just a moment, and then sped on.

"Could you see who was in it?" Penny asked, looking frightened. "Was it Mr. Orandi?" She shook her head. "I don't care if he *does* own an art auction house. He could still be a crook."

"I know. But I couldn't see a thing because of the tinted windows."

"Let's get home," Penny said, "and fast."

We arrived at my garage, puffing. It was too cold to stay in the garage and talk, so we went into the kitchen. No one was home. I had just poured two glasses of milk for us when the phone rang. I answered on the second ring.

"Hello," I said.

"Buckworth," a deep voice said, "we know who you are, and we know you have the tiger. We want it back. Put it in a grocery bag and leave it on the bus-stop bench in front of the bakery at exactly seven-thirty tomorrow morning—is that clear?"

"Yes, sir," I answered. Before I thought to say that we *didn't* have it, he hung up.

"Who was that?" Penny asked.

"Someone thinks we have the tiger and wants me to leave it downtown tomorrow morning."

"We'd better call Mr. Irwin," Penny said, pulling out the phone book and looking for the police number.

"I'll be right over," Mr. Irwin said when he heard what had happened.

As soon as he arrived, Mr. Irwin called Mr. Selby, and they decided to set up a stake-out. After they talked, Mr. Irwin asked if I'd be willing to leave a dummy bag on the bench in the morning. "I know it sounds dangerous, but art thieves are a different breed of crook. They usually aren't violent," he said. "Of course, we'll have you surrounded by undercover officers at all times. And we'll have to get your mother's permission."

"I'm starting to feel scared," Penny said.

"Is anyone home at your house, Penny?" Mr. Irwin asked.

"My parents won't be home until about seven o'clock," Penny said. She didn't mention their house-keeper and gardener. Maybe she wanted to stay with us, where the excitement was.

"You'd better stay here, then. I'll call the station and have them send an officer here for the night. We'll see what happens when we make the drop tomorrow—then we'll decide what to do next."

Two hours later, a teenage girl in jeans and a Middleford letter jacket came to our back door. She was carrying a shopping bag and looked like one of the high-

76

school girls who hang out in the shopping malls. "Officer Kane, Metropolitan Police," she said, flashing her badge at Mr. Irwin.

Penny and I looked at each other. Wow. So she wasn't a teenager after all. Good disguise.

"Mr. Selby called our office, and the chief sent me down," Officer Kane said. We all shook hands.

"Have they told you what's going on?" Mr. Irwin asked.

"Pretty much. He sent along these." She pulled a couple of bricks and a woman's wig out of the bag she was carrying. "Does this look like your mother's hair?" she asked me.

"It's the right color, anyway," Penny said.

"Tomorrow morning I'm going to dress in some of your mother's clothes," Officer Kane said, "and I'll drive you in her car down to the drop point. We'll put the bricks in the bag so it has some weight."

"Can I ride along?" Penny asked.

"Not a chance," Mr. Irwin said to her. Then he turned to Officer Kane. "I'd better go back down to headquarters," he said. "I want to make some calls and see why we haven't gotten those faxed mug shots. We need some action—and quick."

"I'll take care of these two," Officer Kane said.

"I'm glad you're here," Mr. Irwin said to her. Officer Kane smiled.

When Mom came home, she and Officer Kane fussed around with clothes and the wig until, if you squinted a bit, the two of them almost looked like twins. By the time they finished, it was after 7:00. Mom called Penny's house to see if her parents were there.

"They're back," she said to Penny.

"I'd better drive her," Officer Kane said to Mom. "The thieves may be watching her house, too."

"I'll ride along," I said.

"You lock yourself in when we leave," Officer Kane said as Mom handed her the keys to our car.

"You have to wiggle the gearshift lever to get it to start," Mom told Officer Kane. "Chad knows how."

We dropped Penny at her house. Officer Kane walked Penny to the door. Mrs. Palmer, Penny's mom, gave Officer Kane the weirdest look. She seemed to think it was Mom but wasn't sure.

When we pulled up beside our garage, our back door was wide open.

"Mom's gone!" I gasped. "Something's happened!"

"How do you know?" Officer Kane asked, getting out of the car.

"Because she'd never leave the back door standing open like that!"

"Maybe she just walked to the Jiffy Stop for a gallon of milk," said Officer Kane.

"She still wouldn't leave the door standing open. And besides, Mom hardly ever walks after dark." We hurried in. "Mom!" I yelled. No answer. I hunted through the clutter on the kitchen table and looked under the magnets on the refrigerator door. "She always leaves a note—and there's no note here."

"Come with me," Officer Kane said, and went to the front hall closet. I didn't understand what she was doing. She ruffled through the coats she and Mom had tried on earlier. "If your mom *had* gone out, which coat would she have worn?"

"That one." I put my finger on the shoulder of a coat. "Or maybe that one."

"She didn't even take a coat," said Officer Kane, sounding worried. She went to the phone and called the police station, asking them to put out an APB—all-points bulletin—on Mom. She mentioned the black Mercedes and described Mom in detail.

"Now we'll just have to wait," she said. "My fault, Chad. I should never have left her alone. I'm sorry."

A half-hour later, the phone rang again. Officer Kane told me to answer. It was the same voice as before. "We got your mother, Buckworth, just so there's no tricks. Tomorrow morning. Bring the tiger."

"Let me talk to my mom."

When Officer Kane heard me say that, she shot over to my side and put her ear next to mine so she could hear. We heard the man say, "Let her say hello."

"Hi, Chad," I heard Mom's voice say from a distance. "I'm okay."

She must have tried to say something else, but it was muffled. "Tomorrow, seven-thirty," the man said. "No tricks."

"Bring my mom along or no deal," I said, just like in the movies. I don't know where I got the courage to say that. I'm not sure he heard me, anyway. I think he had already hung up.

"This is ridiculous," Officer Kane said. "They should have had your line tapped by now. Small-town cops." She called the station. "Get Irwin and Selby over here right now," she said angrily. "Mrs. Buckworth has been kidnapped, and we've already had a call. So *hurry up with that phone tap,* and notify the FBI."

After she had hung up, she took a deep breath and said gently, "Kidnapping makes this FBI business, Chad. We'll get help real soon."

I sat down at the kitchen table and put my head in my hands. How could we trade the tiger for Mom when we didn't even *have* it? Officer Kane patted me on the shoulder.

I couldn't decide which to do first, pray or cry.

So I did both at the same time.

A Mom Held for Ransom

Art theft was one thing; kidnapping was another. Now that it was a kidnapping and the FBI was in on it, I couldn't believe how fast everyone moved. Our telephone was tapped. By midnight an FBI agent had joined Officer Kane at our house. He didn't look much like an FBI agent to me—he was just a medium-sized guy with gray hair, dressed in a sport coat and a tie.

"I wish the thieves would call again," Officer Kane said, "now that we're ready."

"It would probably be from a phone booth anyway," the agent suggested. "Not much help."

"It wasn't a phone booth last time," Officer Kane argued. "They didn't have Mrs. Buckworth with them in a phone booth."

The agent shrugged. "Maybe we'll get lucky," he said.

"I hope so," I whispered. *But there's no such thing as luck,* I thought, *just like Penny always says.* I went back to praying for my mom: *It isn't luck we need right now, Lord. It's you. Keep her safe, please, Lord. Help the police to catch the crooks, but even if they don't, let my mom get away safe and sound.*

"Are they checking Mercedes registrations?" the agent asked Officer Kane. "Have they found Orandi?"

She shrugged and didn't answer.

We waited through the night. I didn't get a bit sleepy. Just before dawn someone from police headquarters called and said that Orandi was last seen in Chicago and that his secretary said he *was* indeed in Middleford and that he had come here to appraise a piece of art.

Yeah, I thought. *Like a headless tiger.*

Just before the drop time on Friday morning, the police and the FBI agreed that it might be worse for Mom if the kidnappers were expecting the tiger and found nothing but a sack of bricks on the bus-stop bench. They decided it would be better if we didn't leave anything there, because then the thieves would have to call again, and maybe the police could trace the call. As hard as it was, we waited right through the 7:30 drop time. I was scared sick for my mom. *And it's all my fault, too,* I thought, *for playing "finders, keepers" with that stupid tiger.* No matter how much the gold was worth, my mom was worth more.

The scariest part was that the kidnappers were expecting us to pay her ransom with something we didn't have.

About 8:00 the phone rang again. This time everyone was ready. They told me to answer.

"Hello," I said, my voice cracking.

"Hi, Chad," a familiar voice said brightly, "This is Jay."

"Jay, listen" I said quickly, cutting him off. "Hang up and don't call here again today. I'll tell you why on Monday."

I hung up, trembling a little and surprised at how angry I was at Jay. There's no way he could have known not to call, of course.

We waited. Nobody talked. Ten minutes later the phone rang again. I answered again.

"Listen," the same deep voice said. There were rustling sounds, then Mom came on. "Chad, give them what they want." Suddenly Mom's voice was cut off, and the man's voice came back on. "Same place. Noon."

"Bring Mom along," my voice creaked. "No Mom, no tiger."

"Shut up, brat," the man snapped. "Just bring the tiger—and come alone."

Two minutes after the kidnapper had hung up, the phone rang again. The agent looked at me and nodded toward the phone. I answered again. "Hello?" I whispered.

"FBI. Put our agent on, quick," a voice said.

I handed him the phone. The agent listened for a minute, then hung up the phone. "The phone tap worked. They nailed it. Good thing these guys aren't too smart. They're holding her In a house at 912 South Oak Street. You know that address?" he asked me.

"Sure," I said. "That's only a couple of houses away from where Pedro lives—he's at 932. The city crew's working on the street."

"What are they doing to the street?" the agent asked.

"It's all torn up," I said. "In fact, there's a hole in the street just about in front of that house. It's fenced off."

Officer Kane thought about that a minute then said, "Supposing someone were to put on a flak suit and a helmet and drop into that hole from a city maintenance truck?"

"That might just work," the agent said. "We'll need a periscope, and of course walkie-talkies all round. Let's call the station and get it set up. Oh—another thing. Someone just talked to Selby. That tiger, when the head and the body get back together, is worth about three-quarters of a million dollars."

Officer Kane and I just stared.

Later that morning, I hopped on my bike, the bag with the bricks strapped to my bike rack, and pedaled off toward downtown. I had to do it alone—we'd talked about it a long time, and no one could think of another plan that might work. Even knowing that there were six FBI agents in two cars following along didn't make me feel any less scared. One of the agents, seeing how nervous I was, had said, "Take ten deep breaths." I tried. It didn't help.

I made the drop as quick as I could, and I hadn't gotten half a block away when, taking a quick look back over my shoulder, I saw the black Mercedes pull up at the bench. They'd told me to ride away as fast as I could and not to stop or watch—but I couldn't help it. The two cars squealed in and pinned the Mercedes to the curb. Four agents jumped out with guns and the big man,

84

standing half out the car, just raised his hands and gave up without a peep.

One of the cars of agents picked me up and tried to get me to go back to our house and wait with Officer Kane. "Not while my mom's on Oak Street," I said.

A few minutes later, I was in an FBI car parked on Oak Street, watching a city maintenance truck drive slowly past the big hole in the street. By the time it had passed the hole, Monty Irwin had jumped from the side of the truck into the hole and disappeared. No one from the house could have seen it. "We've also got officers in back of the house, and at the ends of the street too," one of the agents told me.

At twenty minutes past noon, a weasely looking man peeked out of the front door. The agent in our car got on the radio and said, "He's getting nervous in there—Williams, you take that man downtown and book him. Jones, drive that Mercedes up to the corner—*now!*"

"Roger," came a voice over the radio.

"What are you going to do?" I asked the agent.

"The thief inside the house doesn't know we've caught his partner. I'm going to drive the Mercedes up to the front of the house and honk. Maybe he'll come out." He slipped out of the car and walked back toward the corner.

"We should get you out of range," the other agent said to me. "This could get ugly."

"I want to stay here where I can see my mother."

"All right. But you stay in the car, understand? No shouting and no getting out. You just watch, no matter what happens. Okay?"

"Okay," I said.

Five minutes later the agent in the black Mercedes parked on the street in front of the house. He honked twice. Because of the tinted windows, I couldn't see him—but then neither could the man inside with my mom.

After the third honk, the weasely man come out of the house—pushing my mom in front of him, with one hand clamped hard above her elbow. Mr. Orandi wasn't with him. I'd never seen the weasely guy before. Was Mr. Orandi still in the house?

Whoever he was, he had a gun. It was all I could do not to jump out of the car and yell at Mom to shake him off and run. I knew if I did, though, I would mess everything up. The man stood on the front step and shouted toward the car, "Open the back door!"

The agent pushed the back door on the curb side open, but the man with my mother didn't move. After a few seconds, the agent in the car shouted, "Come on! I got the tiger!"

But the weasely man must have sensed that something was wrong. He pushed Mom back into the house and, leaving the front door open just a crack, shouted toward the car, "Step out and let me see you!"

The agent stepped out of the driver's door and, standing behind the car, shouted. "This is the FBI! We have the house surrounded and we have your partner. Let the woman come out first, then you come out."

"Not a chance!" the man shouted. "I came to get that tiger and that's what I want. I'll trade you the woman for the tiger—and then I drive out of town with no one following."

"Give us a minute to talk about it," the agent shouted.

"Open both those car doors," the thief shouted back. "Let me see there's nobody else in the car."

The agent opened the back door on the driver's side, then he walked around the car and opened both doors nearest the curb. "Satisfied?" he asked. He left the front door open but pushed the rear door almost closed but not latched.

Then he went back to the driver's side of the car again and, with his hand held low and hidden from the house, motioned to Monty Irwin to climb out of the hole and crawl into the backseat of the car. Mr. Irwin did just that, keeping low and moving quickly. The tinted windows, of course, kept him hidden.

"Walk away from the car," the crook shouted, "and come back with the tiger."

"We don't have the tiger," the agent shouted back.

"Don't kid me!" the voice said. "I know you have it, and I want it."

"We don't know where it is," the agent shouted. "Let the woman go, then we'll talk about you and the car."

"I want that tiger!" the man shouted back.

Just as the man said "tiger," Penny appeared at the end of the street, riding her bike full speed right into the middle of this whole weird scene. The headless tiger was stuck over the end of one of her handlebars.

Where had she found it?

Obviously she had no idea what she was riding into—except for the agent by the car, the rest of us were still hidden. When she saw the black Mercedes with a man standing by it, she slowed down a little.

Just then the man in the house stepped out of the door and pointed his gun at Penny.

I saw her head turn toward the house; I knew she saw him. Maybe it was having a gun suddenly pointed at her, or maybe it was having a ten-pound weight on her handlebar, putting the bike out of balance—whatever caused it, Penny seemed to lose control of her bike and skidded on some construction sand. The tiger was in the way of one of her brake levers, and she hit the other brake too hard—the front brake. Her bike flipped.

The tiger flew off in one direction and she flew in another. She did a complete flip in the air and landed on her hands and knees, half on the sidewalk and half on the grass.

She scrambled to her feet and brushed the dirt off the palms of her hands. One knee was skinned and bleeding, but she looked okay. Everyone froze. The headless tiger had landed right-side-up on the lawn, between the Mercedes and the house.

"Take the girl and back off!" the thief shouted to the agent. "And tell everyone else to back off, too. I'm going to walk out of here with the woman, pick up the tiger, and we're driving away in the Mercedes. I'll let her go when I'm free."

"I can't let you do that," the agent shouted. "Let her go now, before anyone gets hurt."

"*Move!*" the man screamed. He pushed Mom out on the front steps again and pointed the gun at her.

The agent walked over to Penny and grabbed her by the arm. I couldn't hear what he said to her, but the two of them jogged toward us. He opened the door and helped Penny inside, next to me but stayed outside himself, on the far side of the car from the house. The thief stayed on the porch. He still had a gun pointed at my mother. And there wasn't a thing I could do.

I wanted to scream to God for help.

And yet somehow I knew that, even though I didn't say a word, God understood exactly what I wanted.

The Tiger Strikes

The agent reached inside the window for the police radio microphone. He half-whispered into the microphone, "Don't take any chances," he whispered. "We don't want him to panic and do anything stupid. Monty Irwin's in the back seat of the Mercedes. Wait for him to make his move."

"How's your knee?" I asked Penny.

"It hurts."

"Where did you find the tiger?"

"Jay had it," she whispered. "Had it the whole time. Took it to school to make some dumb casting for his art class. Said he tried a dozen times to call you, and when he finally got through, you told him to hang up. Finally he called me."

"How did you know where we were?"

"Officer Kane was still at your house when I got there. She had the police radio on, and I heard someone say something about '912 Oak Street'. I just took a chance and rode my bike over here. I guess I should have asked a few questions first." Penny was biting the skin at the edges of her fingernails.

"Look," I said. "They're coming out on the lawn."

"If he hurts your mom . . ." Penny said, then her voice trailed off. "Dear God," she finally said.

"Amen," I added.

The man and Mom struggled down the front steps and over to the tiger on the lawn. He reached out with his foot and kicked the tiger up against Mom's ankles. "Pick it up," he barked at her, holding her by the elbow with one hand and pointed the gun at her with the other.

Mom bent over very slowly and picked up the tiger by sticking her hand inside its hollow cavity.

"To the car," the thief ordered her. They moved slowly across the front lawn until they were standing near the front door of the Mercedes. The crook commanded Mom, "Get in and slide across to the other side—you'll drive."

That must have been the chance Monty Irwin was waiting for. From inside the back seat he gave the back door a mighty kick. It swung open fast and hard.

Mr. Irwin must have been hoping the door would hit the thief in the back and startle him enough that he'd drop the gun or let go of Mom.

That didn't happen.

The door missed the crook and banged loudly on its hinges.

The crook heard it—and saw it, too. He was so surprised that he turned toward the car and pointed his gun away from Mom and toward Mr. Irwin.

That's when Mom did it.

Mom had her fist inside the tiger. When she saw the crook turn away, she pulled her arm back and with all her might swung her fist and the tiger at his head. He never saw it coming.

She hit him on the side of the head with a ten-pound gold Mesopotamian tiger. It must have felt like she hit him with all of Mesopotamia—wherever that is. The crook dropped the gun, his hand slipped off Mom's elbow, his eyes rolled up into his head, and his knees buckled. He sank to his knees on the sidewalk, then he flopped over, face-down on the grass.

Suddenly swarms of policemen and agents filled the yard. Monty Irwin was out of the car in an instant and kicked the gun out of reach. But the crook didn't move. "Search the house," one of the policemen shouted. Several of them ran in the front door. An agent handcuffed the unconscious man and told someone to call an ambulance.

Penny and I jumped out of the car. I took her hand and we ran. In seconds, Penny, Mom, and I clasped each other tightly in a three-way hug. We were all crying. "Thank God," Mom kept saying over and over again.

"Yeah," the agent said, smiling at the three of us.

"Shall I take that now, Ma'am?" an agent asked, and Mom suddenly noticed that she still had the tiger on her hand. As she raised it up toward the agent he looked at it and said, "You really flattened that sucker."

At first I thought he meant the crook, which made me laugh in relief. But he meant the tiger—she'd hit the guy so hard the tiger was dented in. Mom laughed, too—until the agent started to pull the tiger off her hand. Then she howled in pain. When her hand was free, she examined it. "I think I've broken my thumb," she said.

Later, when Mom and Penny had been patched up in the emergency room, Penny and Mom and Mr. Irwin and I were at home in our kitchen, drinking cocoa and trying to calm down and warm up. Mom had a hard time making cocoa with a cast on her thumb.

As we sat there talking, the phone rang. Mom answered awkwardly with her left hand, then passed the phone across to Mr. Irwin.

He listened, asked a few questions, and then hung up. "We have them for kidnapping, that's for sure," he said. "If we can prove they're the ones who threw the tiger out onto the roadside, we'll probably have them for grand theft as well."

"Penny and I saw the big guy out there," I said, "but we never saw the other one."

"Too bad," Mr. Irwin said.

"You know, it's kind of funny," I said. "That little guy, the weasely looking one, he looked kind of dark and foreign, but he sure didn't talk like a Pakistani."

The others nodded. But the thought of the smaller man being a Pakistani made me think of something. What was it? Something I was forgetting.

I remembered! I reached into the pocket of my jacket, draped across the back of my chair. Yes—still there. The cigarette package.

"Here!" I shouted, pulling out the cigarette package and holding it up. Then I dumped out onto the table the cigarette stub Penny had found in the ditch on the highway. Mom and Mr. Irwin looked puzzled until Penny and I explained what had happened. Then Mr. Irwin nodded. "Maybe that evidence will help," he said. He picked up the phone and called in orders to search the house and the Mercedes for foreign-made cigarettes.

"Oh, by the way," he said, as he hung up the phone, "The kidnapper hasn't come around yet." He smiled at Mom and said, "You gave him a concussion."

"I hope I didn't hurt him *too* badly," Mom said, holding up the cast on her thumb and trying not to smile.

The front doorbell rang. I opened it for Mr. Selby, the insurance investigator from Lloyds of London.

"I came over to congratulate all of you," he said when he got into the kitchen, "and to thank you."

"You're very welcome," Mom said. "But please don't send us any more golden images," she smiled. "After what we've been through, I like them about as much as Moses did."

We all laughed. "I should tell you all something," Mr. Selby said, "lest you get the wrong impression of an innocent man. Mr. Orandi was working with us the whole time. He was trying to buy back the tiger and then help us catch the thieves. It's ironic, actually—he had managed to set up a meeting with the thieves for the same night Chad and Penny here found the tiger in the ditch. When the thieves saw that they were about to be pulled over for speeding, they panicked and threw the tiger out the window, hoping, I'm sure, to come back and find it later. But our young adventurers found it first. And the rest, as they say, is history."

"Then Mr. Orandi wasn't planning to get into the Mercedes behind the hotel that day," I said to Penny. "He was spying, too?"

"Just like we were," Penny finished my sentence. "Whew! What an adventure."

"The other thing I wanted to tell you," Mr. Selby added, "is this. By next spring, the goldsmiths we us in New York will have cleaned off that idiotic camouflage of black paint—and fixed the dent." He smiled at Mom when he said that. "When they have put the tiger's head and body back together and have it ready to send back to the museum, Lloyds of London would like the three of you to come out and see it as it's supposed to look. We're offering you three an all-expense-paid trip to New York. What do you say?"

"That really sounds like fun," Mom said. "Would you two like that?"

"Yes," Penny and I said together.

There was silence then. Everyone seemed to be thinking about what we had been through.

Mr. Selby broke the silence. "You won't believe where we found the tiger's head when we broke into that apartment in the city."

Before anyone could say anything, Penny said, "I'll bet I know."

Mr. Selby smiled and shook his head. "You could never guess in a million years," he said. He reached into his billfold and pulled out a bill. "I'll give you this genuine British ten-pound note if you can."

"In the freezer," Penny said. And suddenly I remembered those first moments when I picked up that ice-cold body of the wrapped tiger in the ditch.

Mr. Selby groaned as he handed her the money, then said with a twinkle, "You'll have to come to London to spend it."

DON'T MISS ANY OF CHAD AND PENNY'S ADVENTURES!

The Mystery of the Gun in the Garbage
Book 1 $5.99   0-310-39801-0

While searching for pop cans, Chad and Penny find something else—a gun! And when the gun disappears, the mystery only deepens. Even the police seem to be involved. Who can Chad and Penny trust? There's danger, mystery, and cliff-hanging suspense.

The Mystery of the Headless Tiger
Book 2 $5.99   0-310-39811-8

When Chad and Penny pick up a package thrown from a speeding black Mercedes, they discover more than litter—it's a solid gold statue! But when the Mercedes returns, so does trouble. Before it's over, Chad's mom is kidnapped and the Earthkeepers must find new courage and faith.

The Mystery of the Forbidden Forest
Book 3 $5.99   0-310-39821-5

What's going on in Wickner's Woods? Each night a truck goes in full and comes out empty. What's being left behind? To discover the poisonous truth, Chad and Penny turn to an elderly widow for help. She helps them crack the case and escape with their lives—barely.

The Mystery of the Hidden Archer
Book 4 $5.99   0-310-39831-2

Someone, or some thing, is in the Northwoods near the family cabin. A mysterious archer saves a kidnapped woman, but authorities find only bear tracks. When the bear tracks appear as the Earthkeepers are planting trees, Penny coaxes out the truth, helping the kids right an old wrong, and save a life.

HEY KIDS!

Would you like to set up your own Earthkeepers Club?
If you do, just send us a letter and we'll mail you a

FREE!
EARTHKEEPERS MEMBERSHIP CLUB KIT

to help you get your club started.

Send your letter to the address below:

**Earthkeepers Club —B18
Zondervan Publishing House
5300 Patterson Ave., S.E.
Grand Rapids, MI 49530**

Be sure to tell us you want an Earthkeepers Club
Membership and include your name and address
in the letter. And if you'd like to add a note letting us
know which Earthkeepers book you read and what
you thought about it, that would be really great.

Offer available while supplies last.